This book belongs to:

....

For Joanna Mary Woodbridge,
I'm happy that you're you.

ORCHARD BOOKS

First published in Great Britain in 2019 by The Watts Publishing Group

1 3 5 7 9 10 8 6 4 2

A CIP catalogue record for this book is available from the British Library.

ISBN HB 978 1 40835 569 5, PB 978 1 40835 570 1

Printed and bound in China

MIX
Paper from responsible sources
FSC® C104740

Orchard Books
An imprint of Hachette Children's Group
Part of The Watts Publishing Group Limited
Carmelite House, 50 Victoria Embankment, London EC4Y 0DZ

An Hachette UK Company
www.hachette.co.uk
www.hachettechildrens.co.uk

Emma Dodd

Thank you,
mouth,

you smile
and giggle.

Thank you,
toes,

you're great to wiggle.

Thank you,
thumbs,
and fingers
too . . .
There's so much
I can do with you!

Thank you, hands,
you touch and hold.

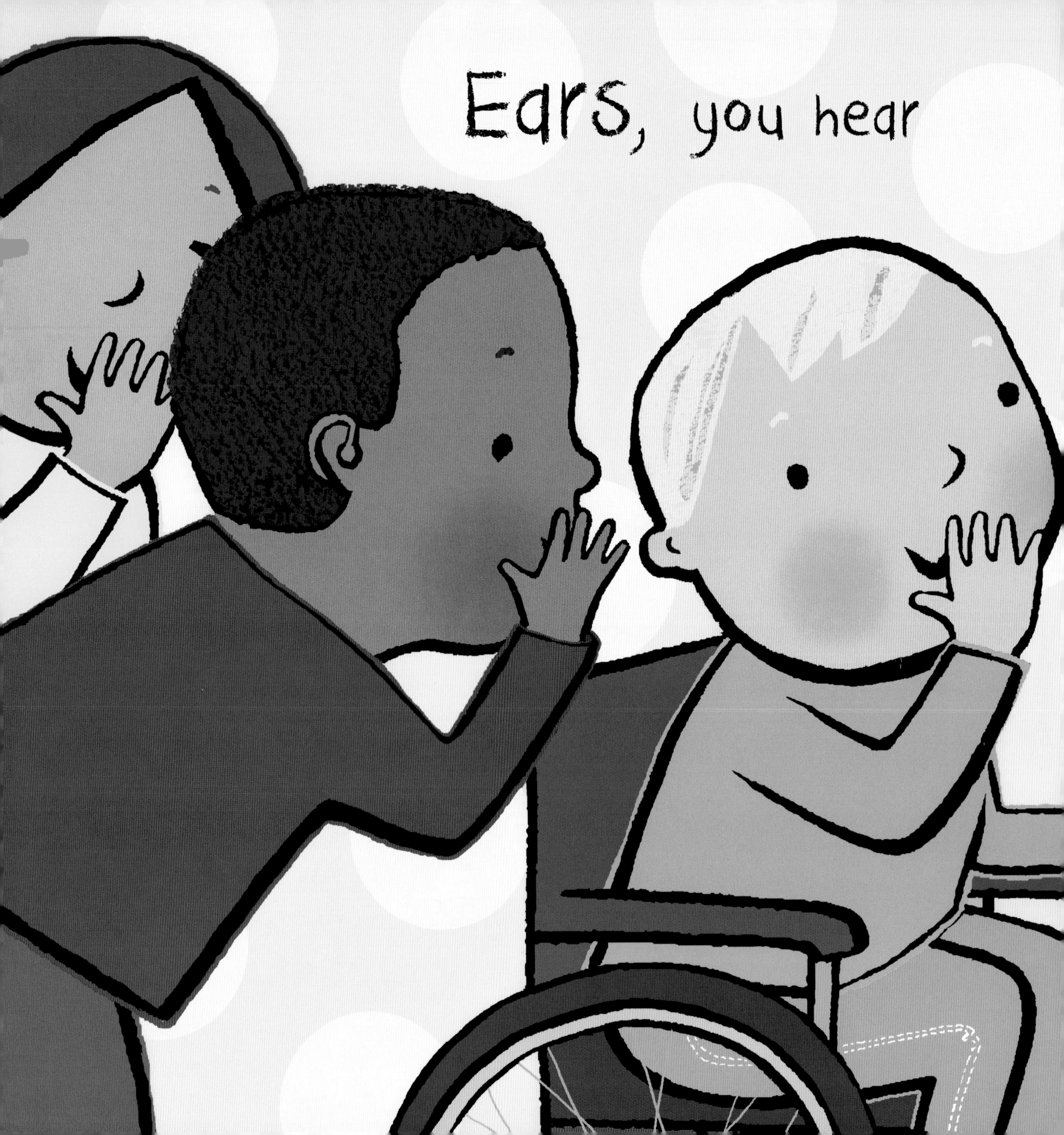
Ears, you hear

the things I'm told.

Thank you, eyes,
you let me see.
Oh, I'm so happy
to be
me!

Head,
you're full
of great
ideas.

Arms, you hug
away my tears.

Thank you, nose,
you let me smell...

you help my tongue
to taste as well.

Legs, you
fold into a lap,
perfect for
a cosy nap.

Lips, you sip and,
teeth, you chew . . .

I eat and drink,
all thanks to you!

And more than
everything above...

Thank you,
heart,

you let me love.

you let me love.